SCOOBY-DOO!
Pirates Ahoy!

Adaptation by Jesse Leon McCann
from the screenplay by Jed Elinoff & Scott Thomas

SCHOLASTIC INC.
New York Toronto London Auckland Sydney
Mexico City New Delhi Hong Kong Buenos Aires

No part of this publication may be reproduced, or stored in a retrieval system, or transmitted in any form or by any means, electronic, mechanical, photocopying, recording, or otherwise, without written permission of the publisher. For information regarding permission, write to Scholastic Inc., Attention: Permissions Department, 557 Broadway, New York, NY 10012.

ISBN-13: 978-0-439-83993-8

ISBN-10: 0-439-83993-9

Copyright © 2006 Hanna-Barbera.
SCOOBY-DOO and all related characters and elements are trademarks of and © Hanna-Barbera. (s06)
Published by Scholastic Inc. All rights reserved.
SCHOLASTIC and associated logos are trademarks and/or registered trademarks of Scholastic Inc.

Designed by Michael Massen

12 11 10 9 8 7 6 5 4 3 2 1   7 8 9 10/0

Printed in the U.S.A.
First printing, October 2006

Scooby-Doo and the Mystery, Inc. gang were going on a cruise to celebrate Fred's birthday! At the port, they met up with Fred's parents, Skip and Peggy Jones.

Sunny St. Cloud, the ship's cruise director, told them they would be sailing to the mysterious Bermuda Triangle!

"No mysteries for a whole week!" Shaggy smiled. "Only buffets and lounging! Ah, this is the life of Shaggy!"

"And Scooby!" Scooby-Doo agreed.

But they were wrong. Soon there were all kinds of mysteries to solve!

But the mysteries were just made up! Captain Cruthers and Sunny St. Cloud were behind them.

"It wouldn't be much of a Bermuda Triangle Mystery Cruise without mysteries!" Sunny said.

"Surprise!" exclaimed Fred's parents. It was their birthday present to Fred.

"Here's another mystery . . . like, what's with the weird castaway?" Shaggy asked.

"Man overboard!" called the captain.

The castaway's name was Rupert Garcia. Rupert was an astrocartographer, an expert in mapping the stars. He said his ship had been sunk by ghost pirates!

"G-g-ghost pirates?!" Scooby and Shaggy didn't like the sound of that one bit!

Moments later, the gang got another surprise.
"Ahoy below!"
It was eccentric billionaire Biff Wellington, riding a jet-pack! Biff was trying to set a new record for the first round-the-world jet-pack flight. He had run out of gas and landed on the cruise ship to borrow some.

"It's time for dinner and the mystery show!" Sunny said.

The light's dimmed, and a voice announced, "Ladies and gentlemen, from lands beyond our consciousness comes . . . Mr. Mysterio!"

Mr. Mysterio hypnotized everyone in the room—except for Scooby and Shaggy!

Meanwhile, out on the deck, the rest of the gang, Skip, and Rupert watched as a mysterious fog enveloped the ship! Fred thought it was just another one of Sunny and the captain's made-up mysteries.

"You don't get it, do you?!" Rupert exclaimed. "It's the ghost pirates! They're coming for me!"

Moments later, a band of ruthless ghost pirates attacked the ship!

"Who dares sail into the Bermuda Triangle?" growled the ghost leader. "Ye've crossed paths with Captain Skunkbeard, the pirate!"

"And Woodenleg Wally," Skunkbeard's helper, a small pirate chimed in.

The ghost pirates rounded up the passengers and took them prisoner on their pirate ship.

Skunkbeard ordered the pirates to sink the cruise ship. The great cannons of the pirate ship boomed, and the ocean liner went under. Scooby and the gang tried to escape, but eventually, the ghost pirates captured them, too!

Soon they had company on the ship. Captain Skunkbeard seemed happy. "Arrg! The phantoms of the triangle's surface! We must be gettin' close."

"Close to where?" Fred asked.

"Like, I don't think I want to find out!" Shaggy said.

"Be strong, me mateys!" Skunkbeard said. "We have finally found the heart of the Bermuda Triangle! At its center is the Heaven's Light!"

"That painting, it must be a map!" Velma said to the gang.

While the pirates were distracted, Daphne was able to cut the gang free. They snuck below deck and found a secret room.

"These look like Captain Skunkbeard's phantoms of the Bermuda Triangle!" Skip said.

Velma nodded. "They seem full-size when projected as holograms!"

"This stuff gives me an idea!" Fred smiled.

"The Heaven's Light is the source of the triangle's amazing power!" Skunkbeard exclaimed. "After tonight, the power will be mine! Now, raise the Heaven's Light from the briny deep!" he ordered.

The crew dropped a mechanical claw and pulled the dripping meteor from the sea.

Suddenly, two aliens appeared on the pirate ship's deck!

"Arrogant humans, you are too weak for the power of the Heaven's Light," said one alien.

"Return it to the sea and release your captives, or pay the consequences!" said the other alien.

The aliens were Daphne and Fred! The pirates saw through their disguises.

"Seize them!" cried Skunkbeard.

Just when things looked hopeless, Scooby-Doo and Shaggy saved the day!

"Like, ahoy, you mangy marauders!" Shaggy shouted.

"Ro-ho-ho!" Scooby cheered as the pirates were bounced around the ships rigging back-and-forth like Ping-Pong balls! Finally, they were scooped up in a big net that Fred had planted.

"Captain Skunkbeard, your jib is up!" Fred said.

Captain Skunkbeard was really billionaire Biff Wellington!

"All my life I wanted to be a pirate. The Heaven's Light will give me the power to control the triangle and travel through history! Now I can be the greatest pirate of all time!"

"Mr. Wellington, where did you get such a crazy idea?" Velma asked.

"From me!" Woodenleg Wally removed his mask— he was Mr. Mysterio! "You used the remote control airplanes to fool Mr. Wellington into believing the Bermuda Triangle legends were true!" interrupted Daphne.

"It was the only way to get him to finance this expedition!" Mr. Mysterio said.

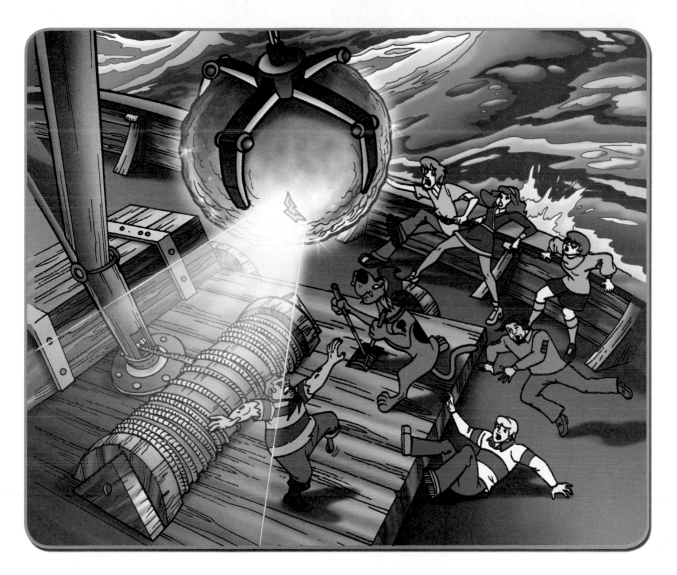

Mr. Mysterio plunged his sword into the meteor.

"The Heaven's Light meteor is solid gold, and now it's all mine!" said Mr. Mysterio. "I'll be richer than you, Wellington!"

Suddenly, the ship began to rock! Waves crashed violently against it!

"It's the Bermuda Triangle!" Biff said. "She wants her meteor back!"

"No!" Mr. Mysterio screamed as Scooby dropped the golden meteor back into the ocean.

Sure enough, the sea became calm again. As the pirate ship sailed back to the safety of the port, Scooby and the gang unmasked the pirates. They were the passengers and crew from the cruise ship! Mr. Mysterio had hypnotized them to act like ghost pirates!

One of the pirates turned out to be Fred's mom, Peggy. When she woke up from her trance, she was so surprised that she almost fell off the ship! Skip tried to save her and almost fell too!

Thinking fast, Velma grabbed a remote control and swooped two planes down to save Fred's parents before they fell in the dangerous waters.

The rest of the trip back was one big party. Fred's parents promised him a better birthday next year.

"Like, some nice, safe cake and ice cream?" Shaggy suggested. Everyone laughed.

"Take us home, Captain!" Fred smiled and saluted Scooby. Scooby saluted back, "Ro-ho-ho and Scooby-Doobie-Doo!"